WITHDRAWN

BEAVERTON CITY LIBRARY
BEAVERTON, OR 97005
MEMBER OF WASHINGTON COUNTY
COOPERATIVE LIBRARY SERVICES

MONSTER HEROES
ZOMBIES AND MEATBALLS

BY BLAKE HOENA
ILLUSTRATED BY DAVE BARDIN

STONE ARCH BOOKS
a capstone imprint

Monster Heroes is published by
Stone Arch Books, a Capstone Imprint
1710 Roe Crest Drive
North Mankato, Minnesota 56003
www.mycapstone.com

Copyright © 2017 Stone Arch Books

All rights reserved. No part of this publication may be reproduced in
whole or in part, or stored in a retrieval system, or transmitted in any
form or by any means, electronic, mechanical, photocopying, recording,
or otherwise, without written permission of the publisher.

Library of Congress Cataloging-in-Publication Data
Names: Hoena, B. A., author. | Bardin, Dave (Illustrator), illustrator.
Title: Zombies and meatballs / by Blake Hoena ; illustrated by Dave Bardin.
Description: North Mankato, Minnesota : Stone Arch Books, a Capstone imprint,
[2017] | Series: Monster heroes | Summary: Brian is a good zombie, so when
the Tofu Brains Deli & Coffee Shop closes, he and his other monster friends
quickly come up with a plan to feed the horde of zombies that is
forming at the hastily renamed Igor's Meatball Brainwich Shop.
Identifiers: LCCN 2016006107 | ISBN 9781496537546 (library binding)
Subjects: LCSH: Zombies--Juvenile fiction. | Monsters--Juvenile fiction.
Heroes--Juvenile fiction. | Friendship--Juvenile fiction. | CYAC: Zombies-
-Fiction. | Monsters--Fiction. | Heroes--Fiction. | Friendship--Fiction.
Classification: LCC PZ7.H67127 Zm 2017 | DDC 813.6--dc23
LC record available at http://lccn.loc.gov/201600610

Book design by: Ted Williams
Photo credit: Krithika Mahalingam Photography (mahalphoto.com), pg 94,
Shutterstock, kasha_malasha, design element

Printed and bound in the United States of America.
009666F16

TABLE OF CONTENTS

MINA (the Vampire)

Mina thinks people taste like dirty socks, so beet juice is her snack of choice. Its red color has fooled her parents into thinking that she's a traditional blood-sucking vampire instead of a superhero hopeful. She has the ability to change into a bat or a mouse at will.

Brian is the brainy one amongst his friends. Unlike other zombies, Brian prefers tofu to brains. No matter what sort of trouble is brewing, Brian always comes up with a plan to save the day, like a true superhero.

BRIAN (the Zombie)

WILL (the Ghost)

Will is quite shy. Luckily he can turn invisible any time he wants because he is a ghost. When Will is doing good deeds, he likes to remain unseen. His invisibility helps him act brave like a real superhero.

With a wave of her wand and a poetic chant, Linda can reverse any magical curse. She hopes to use her magic to help people, just like a superhero would.

LINDA (the Witch)

BRAINS OR BRIAN?

Brian was at his desk working when he heard a strange noise.

"*Braaaiiins!*" came a loud moan.

Brian glanced around his room.

"Did someone just say my name?" Brian whispered.

"*Braaaiiins!*" came the moan again. Only this time, it was louder.

Brian looked up from his homework. He was getting annoyed. He was also getting a little scared.

"Who keeps calling my name?" he asked out loud.

His friends were always saying he studied too much. Maybe they were outside trying to scare him.

"Knock it off you guys," Brian said. "I'm trying to study."

When the moaning continued, Brian realized it wasn't his friends. He went over to his window and looked outside. What he saw scared him more than the moaning.

"Oh, no!" he gasped.

Zombies were everywhere! Hundreds of them lumbered and stumbled about. They destroyed everything in their path, including plants, trees, and mailboxes.

"*Braaaiiins*!" they moaned.

Brian knew that a horde of hungry zombies could be a danger to anyone with a brain.

"*Braaaiiins*!" they moaned louder.

"They are saying '*Braaaiiins*' not '*Briiiaaan*,'" Brian said. "It's true what people say about zombies — they really are hard to understand!"

Brian needed to take action,
and he had to do it fast.

He made his way downstairs
and peeked outside. More and
more zombies filled the streets.

"What is going on?" Brian asked quietly. "The other zombies are usually so well behaved."

"*Braaaiiins!*" they moaned.

Then Brian saw the problem. Down the block was Tofu Brains Deli & Coffee Shop. A CLOSED sign hung outside.

"That's it! They are all hungry!" Brian said.

"*Braaaiiins!*" the zombies moaned.

"I need to call my friends," Brian said. "We need to meet at our hideout right away!"

WHERE ARE THE BRAINS?

Brian's friends were not like other monsters. They did not hurt or scare people. Brian's friends helped people.

They used their special monster powers for good. They wanted to be like superheroes and save the day.

Brian lumbered to the cemetery and climbed up to the hideout. His friends were already there.

Mina hung upside down in one corner. Will floated in another corner. Linda sat in a chair with her pet caterpillar sitting on her shoulder.

"What's wrong?" Linda asked.

"The Tofu Brain Deli & Coffee Shop closed," Brian said.

"No way!" Mina shouted. "I loved that place."

"So did I, but why is that such a big problem?" Will asked. "There are other places to eat."

"But that's where all the zombies eat. Now they are hungry," Brian said. "They are forming a horde."

His friend's eyes went wide with fear. Sure, zombies were slow and clumsy. But a horde of them was unstoppable. They would eat and destroy everything in their path.

"They will look for anyone or anything with a brain," Brian said. "And then . . ."

"This IS a big problem!" Will said.

"It sure is!" Brian said.

Mina held up a map of the city.

"Where do you think they will go?" she asked.

"That's easy," Brian said. "Victor Frankenstein Elementary School has the most brains in town."

Brian looked at the map. He put a finger on Zombie Town. Then he traced the streets leading to the elementary school.

"This is the path they will follow," Brian said.

"How do we stop the horde from getting there?" Will asked.

Brian studied the map. There were stores and restaurants along the way to the school.

"That's it!" Brian said.

"What's it?" Linda asked.

"A trip to the meatball shop, that's what!" Brian said.

"Getting a bite to eat?" Mina said. "That's your brilliant plan?"

"Just trust me," Brian said.

CHAPTER 3

MEATBALL BRAINS

The friends stood outside Randy's Meatball Sandwich Shop.

"The meatballs here are really good," Will said.

"And they kind of look like little brains," Brian said, holding one up. "Now, huddle up, team!"

Brian whispered his plan. They all agreed and got into position.

Linda waved her wand at the restaurant's sign.

"Your name must change," she chanted.

Poof! The sign now read Igor's Meatball Brainwich Shop. Linda's job was done.

Now it was Brian's turn. He joined the zombie horde.

"*Braaaiiins!*" the zombies moaned as they lumbered down the street.

"*Meeeatbaaalls!*" Brian groaned.

"*Braaaiiins!*" the zombies moaned again.

"*Meeeatbaaalls!*" Brian groaned louder.

The zombies kept moaning. Brian kept groaning louder. Soon, the zombies' moans changed to groans. Brian's job was done.

"*Meeeatbaaalls!*" the zombies groaned.

Will tied a string to a meatball. Then he took off his sheet. Now he was invisible.

Will used the meatball on a string to lead the zombies to the sandwich shop. Will pulled the meatball away as soon as the zombies reached for it.

"*Meeeatbaaalls!*" the zombies groaned.

Brian groaned along with them. "*Meeeatbaaalls!*"

Brian and the zombies followed Will right to the restaurant. Will's job was done. Now it was Mina's turn to take over.

Mina quickly made stacks and stacks of meatball sandwiches. Then she changed into a bat. She fluttered about the restaurant.

The horde of zombies entered the shop and attacked the piles of meatball sandwiches.

"*Meeeatbaaalls!*" the zombies groaned.

The friends regrouped outside the sub shop. They watched as the zombies ate every sandwich in sight.

"We stopped them!" Linda said.

"The monster heroes saved the day again," Mina said.

"That's because we make a great team," Brian said.

"We sure do," Will mumbled between bites. "What? Nobody else is hungry?"

DAVE BARDIN

Dave Bardin studied illustration at Cal State Fullerton while working as an art teacher. As an artist, Dave has worked on many different projects for television, books, comics, and animation. In his spare time Dave enjoys watching documentaries, listening to podcasts, traveling, and spending time with friends and family. He works out of Los Angeles, CA.

BLAKE A. HOENA

Blake A. Hoena grew up in central Wisconsin, where he wrote stories about robots conquering the moon and trolls lumbering around the woods behind his parents house. He now lives in Minnesota and continues to write about fun things like space aliens and superheroes. Blake has written more than fifty chapter books and graphic novels for children.

ZOMBIE'S GLOSSARY

brain—a zombie snack; also, the organ in a person's head that controls bodily functions and is used for thinking

cemetery—a hang-out for zombies; also, a place where dead people are buried

hideout—a secret place

horde—a large group of people (or zombies)

lumber—to move in a slow, awkward way; the only way zombies move

tofu—food made from soybeans, often used as a meat substitute (this has nothing to do with zombies)

THINK ABOUT IT

1. Why do you think the author chose to name the main zombie Brian, which is spelled almost the same as "brain"?

2. Within this story, several place names are used, such as Zombie Town and Frankenstein Elementary School. How does including these names help the setting of the story?

3. Each of the characters plays a part in the plan to stop of the horde of zombies. What would have happened if one of the characters failed to do their part?

WRITE ABOUT IT

1. What would you do if you saw a horde of zombies? Make a list describing your plan.

2. Zombies are not pretty creatures. Write a detailed description of a zombie, and use at least five character traits.

3. The story ends with the zombies happily eating meatball sandwiches. What happens when they get hungry again? Write a paragraph about what you think will happen.

THE FUN DOESN'T STOP HERE!

Discover more at
www.capstonekids.com

Find cool websites and more books like this one
at www.facthound.com. Just type in the Book ID:
9781496537546 and you're ready to go!